For my husband,
Peter, and the dear
family he has brought
into my Life; Mom
"Berta" and all of the
Banks and Foitos.

Wallace, Nancy Elizabeth.
Tell-a-bunny / written and illustrated by Nancy Elizabeth Wallace.
First Edition
p.   cm.
Summary: As one bunny passes the message on to the next, Sunny's plans for a surprise birthday party
for Earl undergo some changes.
ISBN 1-890817-29-5
[1. Communication Fiction. 2. Parties Fiction. 3. Birthdays Fiction. 4. Rabbits Fiction.]   I. Title.
PZ7.W15875Te   2000
[E] — dc21
99-36456   CIP

Text and illustrations copyright 2000 by Nancy Elizabeth Wallace
The Illustrations in this book were prepared with cut paper.

Creative Director: Bretton Clark
Designed by Aaron Braun
Letter Art by Jessica Wolk-Stanley
Editor: Margery Cuyler

For games, links and more, visit our interactive Web site:

www.winslowpress.com

Tell •A• Bunny

Written and illustrated by
Nancy Elizabeth Wallace

WINSLOW PRESS

DELRAY BEACH, FLORIDA • NEW YORK

Earl's birthday was tomorrow.
Sunny wanted to give him a surprise party.
She made a list of all the things their friends could do.
Then she phoned Gloria.

Ring, Ring, Ring.

Sunny whispered, "Hello, Gloria, it's Sunny.
Tomorrow is Earl's birthday. I want to give him
a surprise party at six o'clock.
Tell Libby to bring her Yummy-Plummy Tan Cake.
Tell Mugsey to bring six spoons and his blue plates.
Tell Baxter to bring a large blanket.
Tell Lottie to bring her soccer ball.
Gloria! Bye! I have to hang up 'cause here comes Earl!"

"Sunny said 'buy.' I wonder what she wants me to buy for the party?" said Gloria. "I'd better go shopping."

Gloria went to the store and picked out a gift.

When Gloria got back, she telephoned Libby.

Ring, Ring, Ring.

"Libby, it's Gloria. There's a sunrise birthday party for Earl tomorrow at six. Sunny wants to know if you would make your delicious Yummy-Tummy Pancakes.
Tell Mugsey to bring six spoons and his blue plates.
Tell Baxter to bring a big blanket.
Tell Lottie to bring her soccer ball."

Crunch, Crunch, Crunch.
Libby finished her sixth bag of potato chips.
"Sure thing," she said.

Libby went to the pantry and gathered together
the ingredients for pancakes.

Then Libby telephoned Mugsey.

Ring, Ring, Ring.

"Mugsey, it's Libby. There's a birthday party for Earl tomorrow at six A.M., sunup. Please pick some tunes and bring your new plates. Oh, and bring some potato chips.
Tell Baxter to bring the pig blanket.
Tell Lottie to bring her soccer ball."

Mugsey shouted, "I WILL."

"Shoup, Shoup, Dooo-Whaah," Mugsey sang.
"It will be fun to pick tunes. I'll bring a jar
of tomato dip and wear my new skates!"

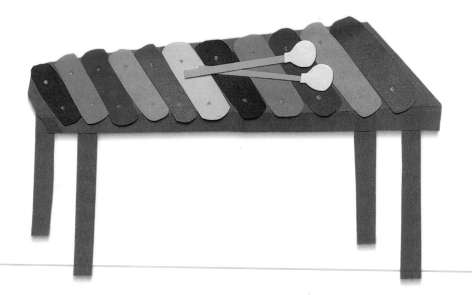

Then Mugsey telephoned Baxter.

Ring, Ring, Ring.

"Hi, Baxter, it's Mugsey. There's a party at Earl's
tomorrow at six o'clock in the morning.
Please bring a big banquet and
tell Lottie to bring her soccer ball."

Baxter had the hiccups.
He shouted back, "O-(hiccup)-**KAY**."
"A get-together at sunup?" Baxter grumbled.
"What a silly idea. And they want me (hic) to
bring a banquet? That's a lot of food!"

Baxter went into the kitchen.
He squeezed and chopped, he diced and sliced.
He put together a banquet.

Then Baxter telephoned Lottie.

"Hello, Lot."

"Lottie is in the shower," said her father.

"Would you tell her Baxter called? Someone had the silly idea to have a party at sun-(hic)-rise at Earl's tomorrow. Would you tell Lot-(hic)-tie to bring her soc-(hic)-cer ball?"

"I will tell her," said her father.

"Dumpling," called Lottie's father. "Baxter phoned.
He said that there is a 'Silly Sunrise Party'
at Earl's tomorrow and to bring a lot
of your socks and balls."

"Cool," said Lottie.

♥ ♥ ♥ ♥ ♥

Lottie went to her room to get ready for the party.

Very early the next day,
everyone went to Sunny and Earl's house.

Sunny and Earl woke up and heard music.
They tiptoed downstairs.
They peeked into the living room.

"Happy Birthday, Earl!!!!!"

Earl made a wish on the stack of Yummy-Tummy Pancakes.

Everyone ate and laughed and sang and played games.
Earl opened the gift from his friends.
Then everyone went home.

"Sunny, this was the best birthday surprise party
ever!" said Earl. "How did you do it?"
Sunny looked at her list and wondered, too.

THE END

...or was it?

Ring, Ring, Ring.